Advent OF THE Robber Pig

CONTENTS

The Robber Pig
and the Green Eggs

The robber pig stole a bottle
of milk from the king's milk box.

"I shall drink this milk down
by the mud," said the robber pig.

As he ran, he left footprints
in the mud.

"Woof, woof, woof!" barked
the king's royal bloodhound,
Merriman.

"Bother!" muttered the robber pig.
"I must get rid of the evidence."

The robber pig quickly drank
the milk and threw the bottle
away. Being a pig, he drank
too quickly and gave himself
the hiccups.

"Now to hide," he said.
"Shall I hide in the grass
and pretend I'm a rabbit?"

He looked in the grass.
There, beside him, was a nest
of green eggs.

"This is my lucky day!"
cried the robber pig. "First milk
and now eggs."

"Woof, woof, woof!" howled
Merriman.

The robber pig hiccuped.

"I'll eat the eggs later," he said.
"But I won't hide in the grass.
I might squash them.
I'll hide in the mud and pretend
to be a mud snake."

Being a pig, the robber pig
didn't mind mud. He snuggled
down deep.

Every time he hiccuped,
the mud shook.

"Woof, woof, woof! The footprints lead right here to these, Your Majesty," cried Merriman, pointing to the pig's eyes.

The king looked at the eyes. He looked at the ears. He looked at the tail.

"It's the robber pig!" he said.

"No," cried the robber pig. "I'm not the robber pig. I'm a mud snake."

"Get out of that mud and show yourself!" cried the king.

"Come and get me," said the robber pig.

"I know it's you!" said the king. "I can see the milk bottle."

"The milk bottle doesn't count,"
said the pig. "Can you see
the milk?" He hiccuped,
and all the mud shook.

The eggs in the nest shook, too.
Out hatched a little mud snake.
It looked up.

"Mother!" it said to the king.

"I'm not your mother!"
said the king. "There's
your mother. She's lying
in the mud."

The robber pig hiccuped
again, and more eggs
hatched.

"Mother! Mother!"
cried the little snakes.
"Darling Mother,
get us something
to eat. We're hungry.
Get us lots of mud flies."

The snakes wrapped themselves around the robber pig's snout. They tickled his ears and swung on his tail.

"What a dear little curly cousin!" they cried to his tail.

"Come on, Merriman. Home we go!" laughed the king.

So the robber pig had to catch
flies for fifty little mud snakes.
He had to feed them on flies
until they were all grown-up.
And he had terrible hiccups
the whole time!

The Robber Pig
and the
Ginger Drink

Mrs Lockett lived on one side
of the hill. She was a good cook.

On the other side of the hill
lived the robber pig. He cooked
very badly. All of his baking dishes
were burned black.

One day, Mrs Lockett made a pie and left it out to cool.

Along came the robber pig, who stole the pie.

Mrs Lockett made a cake and left it out to cool.

The robber pig stole the cake, too.

"Diddle, diddle, dumpkin!" sighed Mrs Lockett. "I'm not going to bake any more. I shall make some of Granny's fizzy-whizzy ginger drink instead."

She got out her granny's recipe book and made fizzy-whizzy ginger drink.

Fizzy-Whizzy Ginger Drink

1.5 litre plastic bottle
2 tablespoons warm water
½ teaspoon sugar
¼ teaspoon yeast granules

1 cup sugar
juice of 2 lemons
rind of 2 lemons
2 teaspoons ground ginger

1. Put ½ teaspoon sugar in warm water to dissolve, add yeast, then stir. Put in warm place.
2. Pour 1 cup of boiling water over rind and juice, cup of sugar, and ginger. Leave for 10 minutes. Strain liquid into bottle. Top up with cold water.
3. When yeast foams, pour into bottle. Put lid on bottle, gently shake, and leave in warm place until bottle becomes firm (12 hours to 3 days later).
4. Chill bottle, then open very carefully!

"Why isn't she baking anything?"
the robber pig asked.
"If I were good at baking,
I'd bake all the time."

The ginger drink fizzed and
whizzed in its bottles and tried
to push the corks out.

The robber pig crept closer
to see what was going on.
"She's got something
in the kitchen," he said greedily.
He made up a very wicked plan.
He knocked on the front door.

Mrs Lockett went through
the dining room, along the long
hall, and to the front door.
While she did this, the robber
pig ran around to the back of the
house and went into the kitchen.

"Where is the food?"
asked the robber pig greedily.

The fizzy-whizzy ginger drink
heard him. It pushed
at its corks. BANG went
one bottle of ginger drink.
BANG went another.
The first cork hit
the pig on the snout.
The second cork hit
his curly tail. He thought
he had been shot.

"Help! Help!" he squealed.
"She has hidden a hunter
in her kitchen."

Mrs Lockett heard the ginger drink exploding. She went back down the long hall, through the dining room, and into the kitchen.

"No one here!" she said.

The robber pig was running up the hill, his tail curled up tight with terror.

Mrs Lockett saw the bubbly ginger drink.

"What lovely fizzy-whizzy ginger drink I have made!" she cried.

So she sat out in the sun and drank a glass of it!

Beautiful Pig

One morning, the robber pig looked at himself in the mirror.

"How beautiful I am!" he said. "I must go out and let everyone else see how beautiful I am."

So he tied a ribbon on his tail and set out into the world.

First he met a dog.

"Hello, Dog!" said the pig. "This is your lucky day! You may look at me for as long as you like and see how beautiful I am."

"Beautiful?" cried the dog.
"Your nose is not pointed.
Your tail is not feathery.
You are very plain."

"What nonsense!" said the pig,
and he ran off down the road.

23

Next he met a cat.

"Hello, Cat!" cried the pig. "This is your lucky day! Take a look at me and see how beautiful I am."

"Beautiful?" said the cat. "Where are your whiskers? Where are your paws? You are very plain."

"What nonsense!" said the pig, and he ran off down the road.

Then he met a wolf.

"Hello, whoever you are!" cried the pig. (He had never seen a wolf before.) "See how beautiful I am."

"You ARE beautiful!" said the wolf. Come here and let me look at your beauty." The wolf took out his knife and fork.

"Oh no!" cried the pig.
He knew something was wrong.
"You must look, look, look –
not cook, cook, cook!"

He ran off down the road.
He had to go under twenty-seven
hedges before he got away
from the hungry wolf.

The pig sat down sadly
and cried all down his snout.

"Maybe I am just a plain pig
after all!" he said to himself.

"Hello, there!" said a soft, grunting voice. "Who are you, Fascinating Stranger?"

"I am the robber pig, but do not look at me. I am very plain."

"Oh no!" said the soft, grunting voice. "Your snout is perfectly perfect, and I love the ribbon on your tail. You are very, very beautiful."

"That's what I think, too!"
said the robber pig, looking up.
"Oh, I thought I was beautiful,
but you are more beautiful still.
We must get married!"

"Only if you give up
being a robber pig,"
said the black-and-white pig.

So the pigs got married and
had ten little piglets. Strange
to say, they were all beautiful –
as beautiful as a pig can be!

And the robber pig gave up
his robbing ways!

FROM THE AUTHOR

Sometimes I imagine being a robber pig myself. I imagine leaping into my car and making a quick getaway. But, like the robber pig, I wouldn't get very far. I would run out of petrol. The robber pig stories are like my real life.

Margaret Mahy

FROM THE ILLUSTRATOR

People say that pigs are very clever and are always getting into mischief, just like the pig in these stories. One day, I would like to have a pet pig, but, for now, I have my hands full with two cats and three hens living with me in the middle of the city of Sydney, Australia.

Rodney McRae